Special thanks to Venetia Davie, Ryan Ferguson, Charnita Belcher, Tanya Mann, Julia Phelps, Sharon Woloszyk, Nicole Corse, Darren Sander, Rita Lichtwardt, Debra Zakarin, Karen Painter, Stuart Smith, Carla Alford, Julia Pistor, Renata Marchand, Michelle Cogan, Shareena Carlson, Kris Fogel, Rainmaker Entertainment and Conrad Helten and Lilian Bravo

randomhousekids.com

ISBN 978-0-553-53917-2 (trade) — ISBN 978-0-553-53918-9 (ebook)

Printed in the United States of America
10 9 8 7 6 5 4 3 2 1

Adapted by Mary Tillworth

Based on the screenplay by Marsha Griffin and Kacey Arnold

Illustrated by Ulkutay Design Group

A GOLDEN BOOK • NEW YORK

It was a big day at the gymnasium. Top gymnasts from around the world were competing in the championship qualifying trials.

The onlookers cheered as a lone gymnast swooped through the air, executing a perfect backflip, round-off, triple-twist combination.

"For a team of one, Patricia's pretty stiff competition!" exclaimed Barbie's teammate Renee.

"Her margin for error is infinitesimal," moaned their other teammate Teresa.

"You know what that means," Barbie said. "Pandora's Pyramid!"

Pandora's Pyramid was a sequence of twists and jumps that ended with Barbie performing a triple somersault onto Teresa's and Renee's shoulders.

The girls began their routine. Barbie could feel herself getting more and more nervous. Instead of completing the pyramid, Barbie somersaulted through the air, missed her last rotation, and landed with a thud on the mat!

"Ugh!" Barbie said after the trial. "I totally psyched myself out."

"Don't be so hard on yourself," Teresa told her. "We still qualified for the championship finals!"

Just then, Renee's phone beeped. "Auntie Zoe just invited us to a picnic to celebrate getting into the finals."

The girls followed Auntie Zoe's directions. As they sat down for their picnic, a sign behind them suddenly slid open, revealing a secret entrance!

"Let's go check it out!" said Barbie.

Inside, they discovered a secret headquarters filled with blinking screens and high-tech equipment.

"Welcome to I3, the International Intelligence and Innovation Agency," called a familiar voice. It was Auntie Zoe! She was the head of I3 and had decided to recruit the girls as secret agents.

Renee gasped. "I can't believe you're head of an international intelligence agency!" Her sweater-knitting, cat-loving aunt was way cooler than she had imagined!

"I've been watching you girls compete since you were little. I've never seen such raw talent," Auntie Zoe explained. "And I need you for a special mission. A jewel thief has stolen six of nine gems that can be used to power a dangerous electromagnetic pulse weapon, or EMP, for short."

"This is our chance to do something really awesome and make a difference. We're in!" declared Barbie.

Auntie Zoe introduced the girls to a gruff man in a black suit. "This is Agent Dunbar. He will be your training specialist."

Agent Dunbar led the girls to a lab where a young man was tinkering with robot pieces.

"This is Lazslo, our resident inventor," Agent Dunbar said. "He's behind every gadget, weapon, and disguise used by our agency."

"Did you make this arm on a 3-D printer with glass fiber and nylon composite?" Teresa asked Lazslo.

"Yeah. How'd you know that?" Lazslo responded.

"I've been toying with some robot designs of my own," Teresa said.

A robotic dog trotted up to Barbie, with a purring robotic kitten close behind.

"Meet Percy and Violet, my state-of-the-art techbots," Lazslo said proudly. "Percy will be your very own bot. He's indispensable when it comes to surveillance and gadgetry in the field."

Agent Dunbar led the girls to the training room for their first exercise.

"Piece of cake!" exclaimed Renee as she rappelled down a multistory wall using a purse zip line.

"Unless the rope breaks or our safety harnesses fail," groaned Teresa.

Barbie swung down by her friend. "You got this, T. Just breathe."

Teresa looked into Barbie's eyes and nodded. In unison, the girls leaped off the wall and glided safely to the ground.

The next task was to get through a room full of moving lasers without triggering an alarm. Barbie studied the shifting beams. "I think the handspring combination from our gymnastics routine might do the trick!"

The girls launched into a series of leaps, dives, and flips that carried them safely past the lasers.

Back in the invention lab, the girls tested smart-watch communicators, makeup brushes that could transform their faces, and three supercharged motorcycles.

Barbie picked up a plain-looking stick. As she twisted it, energy beams shot out from each side. "Cool!"

Lazslo handed her a bracelet. "It's a Gymnastic Launching Innovative Spy Stick, or G.L.I.S.S. If you wear this bracelet receiver, you can throw the stick and it'll come back to you like a boomerang."

"It's all amazing!" exclaimed Teresa.

Just then, the smart-watch communicators beeped. Barbie pressed a button, and a video image of Auntie Zoe appeared. "Satellite surveillance has just detected a security breach inside the penthouse owned by billionaire gem collector Griffith Pitts. Girls, it's go time!"

Lazslo met the girls outside with their motorcycles and matching helmets. "They're hairdo helmets—they leave your hair better than when you put them on!"

Barbie put on her helmet and revved her motorcycle as Percy hopped in the sidecar. "Spy Squad, let's go!"

Barbie and her friends entered Griffith Pitts's huge loft, where they discovered the jewel thief pocketing a gem!

Barbie and her friends sprang into action, twisting and flipping to avoid the billionaire's laser maze security.

"You're mine now!" shouted Barbie as they gained on the robber. Just as they were closing in, the thief flew over a railing and glided down a glass skyscraper using a high-tech zip line.

Barbie, Teresa, and Renee deployed their purse zip lines, but Teresa hesitated, frozen with fear.

"You've got to stop looking down!" Renee said.

"I can't!" Teresa wailed.

"You can do this," Barbie told Teresa patiently. "It's just like we practiced. Just breathe."

The three girls looked at one another. They all took deep breaths and jumped—right into one another! The zip lines tangled together, and the girls ended up dangling sixty feet off the ground.

"Wish I could hang around, but you know me—places to go, things to steal!" The thief hopped on a motorcycle and zoomed off.

The girls untangled themselves and returned to headquarters, where Auntie Zoe was waiting for them. "Let's just chalk this up to rookie jitters, shall we?" she said. "Tomorrow night, the National Museum is holding an invitation-only gala for its exhibition of ancient gemstones."

Teresa set her smart watch for the gala. The Spy Squad would be ready!

The next day, Barbie practiced using the G.L.I.S.S. As she whirled and leaped, Auntie Zoe came in to watch.

Barbie launched herself so high, she could have easily completed the Pandora's Pyramid move. "Wish I had this at trials!" she laughed.

Auntie Zoe smiled. "Have you ever tried visualizing? I call this technique 'see it—then be it.' Picture yourself doing something. And then you can do it!"

"I'll try!" promised Barbie.

That night, while sleek black limousines rolled up to the main entrance of the National Museum, three motorcycles darted into a service alley. Barbie and her friends had decided to infiltrate the invitation-only gala disguised as chefs. As they snuck into the kitchen, Percy scurried through a side entrance to gather information.

Soon the girls heard Percy's voice on their smart watches. "I'm in position. You're clear!"

Once inside the museum ballroom, Barbie and her friends had to blend in with the gala guests. In a shower of sparkles, their chef disguises transformed into beautiful ball gowns—only their outfits included jewelry-set communicators, tech glasses, and bracelet scanners!

"We have a breach!" Percy growled over their communicators. "Northwest corner!"

Barbie nodded. "Copy that. We're on our way."

The girls hurried up a grand staircase to the northwest corner of the museum. But when they arrived, there was no one in sight.

Renee tapped on her tech glasses. "The security system has been hacked!"

Teresa checked her bracelet scanner. "Percy's frequency has been scrambled."

Barbie groaned. "This was just a trick to draw us away from the gems!"

The girls rushed through the gem exhibit. As they searched the room, a figure stepped out of the shadows. It was the jewel thief, holding a gem!

"This ends now!" shouted Barbie as she and her friends transformed their ball gowns into spy suits and took off after the thief.

"I don't know why you try to keep up with me," sneered the thief before performing a daring midair twist.

"Was that a triple Arabian twist?" Barbie whispered.

They watched helplessly as the thief reached the top of the sculpture and fired a zip line, propelling her through the glass roof of the museum. Barbie and her friends had failed—again!

Back at headquarters, Auntie Zoe had more bad news. "We just learned that the gem we had in evidence is now missing."

"Unfortunately, you won't be the ones to retrieve it," Agent Dunbar said with a smirk.

"We're being fired?" Renee gasped.

Auntie Zoe nodded sadly. "The director of national intelligence has decided to terminate your training. The stakes are just too high now. I'm sorry, girls."

The next day, the girls went back to the gymnasium to practice for the championships. As they warmed up, Barbie saw her sister Chelsea crash into her teammate Mila during a tumbling move.

"I keep messing up!" Chelsea moaned as Barbie helped her to her feet.

Barbie hugged Chelsea. Suddenly, she remembered Auntie Zoe's advice: "The next time you get nervous about a move, visualize it exactly how you want it, then do it. See it—then be it!"

Chelsea took a deep breath and concentrated. She tried the tumbling move again—and landed beautifully!

As Barbie congratulated her sister, Patricia walked onto the mat and executed a daring tumbling combination.

"Was that a triple Arabian twist?" Barbie gasped.

Patricia nodded smugly. "I don't know why you try to keep up with me."

Suddenly, Patricia's words—and her moves—all made sense to Barbie. "You're the jewel thief!" she exclaimed.

"So you found me," Patricia said with a smirk. She started to run for the exit. "Too bad finding and catching aren't the same thing!"

Luckily, Lazslo had allowed the girls to keep their spy gadgets, disguises, and motorcycles for one more day. Soon Barbie and her friends were chasing Patricia through traffic, weaving through honking cars and huge semitrucks, all the way to . . . l3!

Inside the secret agency headquarters, the girls discovered a shocking surprise. Agent Dunbar had stolen plans from I3 to create the EMP weapon—and Patricia had been helping him steal the gems to power it!

"Patricia, it's not too late," Barbie told the talented gymnast. "You could be part of our team. We actually care about you."

"Silence!" thundered Dunbar. Before they could act, Barbie and her friends were captured by robots.

"They overlooked *me* for your precious Auntie Zoe." Agent Dunbar smiled. "That's why I'm going to use the EMP weapon to cripple the agency, and I'll blame it on your aunt." He cackled evilly. "Who needs to run an agency when you can run the world!"

Dunbar offered Patricia the last gem to place in the EMP weapon. "Would you like to do the honors?"

Patricia slowly backed away. "Uh, no thanks. I just wanted to make some extra cash. I'm not into the whole world domination thing."

Patricia dove under Dunbar's robots and took off down the hallway.

"You watch the girls," Dunbar called to his robots as he headed toward the weapon room with the final gem.

Barbie kicked the robot restraining Teresa. Teresa broke free and knocked over the robot holding Renee, sending it crashing into the robot clutching Barbie. The girls were free!

"You two find Lazslo and get working on reprogramming the robots," Barbie told Renee and Teresa. "I'm going after Dunbar."

Barbie tried to stop the evil agent, but Dunbar's robots swarmed her. "You'll never get away with this!" Barbie cried.

Agent Dunbar laughed. "Oh, but I already have."

"Not so fast!" A familiar figure leaped out from behind the EMP weapon. It was Patricia! Using her swift gymnastic moves, Patricia easily kicked her way through the robots that had captured Barbie.

"Why the sudden team spirit?" Barbie asked Patricia.

"Let's just say having people who care might not be the worst thing," answered Patricia. Side by side, the two girls destroyed Dunbar's robots as they got closer and closer to the evil agent.

Just as Teresa and Renee reprogrammed the last robot, Barbie took down Dunbar with a mighty kick!

The reprogrammed robots quickly captured Dunbar, but the EMP weapon was still active. "We have to contain the EMP weapon before it emits a pulse!" shouted Teresa.

"If we can detach just one of the gems, we can stop this thing from going off." Barbie closed her eyes and concentrated, visualizing what she and her teammates would need to do. "I've got it!" she shouted. "Pandora's Pyramid!"

"See it—then be it." Barbie repeated Auntie Zoe's advice. She took a deep breath. Barbie flipped and twisted, landing perfectly. As her friends held her up, Barbie used the G.L.I.S.S. and pried up the gem until it went flying! The weapon was deactivated—and the world was saved!

"Guess I underestimated you," Patricia confessed to the girls as Agent Dunbar was dragged away.

Renee smiled. "You underestimated a lot!"

"Are you going to tell me that perspective is one of those things that friends are good for?" Patricia asked.

Barbie hugged her new friend. "Seems that way, doesn't it?"

Auntie Zoe congratulated Barbie and her friends. "You all should be proud of yourselves. What you did today was nothing short of remarkable."

As the girls celebrated, Teresa checked her watch. It was almost time for the championship finals! "Guys, we've gotta bounce!"

Auntie Zoe nodded. "All right, but afterward I want to talk to you girls about coming back to the agency. . . ."

The girls raced back to the championship finals. Barbie closed her eyes and remembered Auntie Zoe's words again. "See it—then be it," she whispered. She took a deep breath and ran, then tumbled and twisted through the air—right onto her teammates' shoulders! They had nailed Pandora's Pyramid and won the finals!

As the crowd went wild, Barbie gave her teammates a hug. She knew that she could be and do anything she wanted—with her teammates by her side.

MISSION COMPLETE